# The Remarkable Riderless Runaway Tricycle

Revised Edition

Bruce McMillan

3/10/95
To Andrew
Who met my tricycle

APPLE ISLAND BOOKS

shapleigh, me. 04076
1985

# For Mom and Dad

**In its own small way
may this book help
the memory of
Butch
live on.**

**Originally published by
Houghton Mifflin
1978**

McMillan, Bruce.
  The remarkable riderless runaway tricycle.

  SUMMARY: A tricycle relegated to the trash heap
manages its own salvation.
  [1.  Bicycles and bicycling—Fiction]  I.  Title.

ISBN 0-934313-00-8

Jason was feeling sad.  His tricycle was gone.  His parents had thrown it away because they thought it was too rickety and worn-out.

The trash man had picked it up and taken it to the Kennebunkport Dump.

Soon it would be plowed under by the bulldozer.

With Ernest, the dump man, at the controls the bulldozer hissed and
lurched forward, scooping up a bucketful of trash and heading to the big pit.

But Ernest's hands slipped on the controls and the tricycle fell out.

Jason's tricycle began to move. "Oh no!" bellowed Ernest. "This trash never goes where I want it to go."

"Stop! Stop!" he yelled as he chased the tricycle. "You're my trash!" But the faster he ran the faster the tricycle rolled.

It raced along at full tricycle speed.  At the end of the dump road it careened around the corner and onto Beachwood Avenue.

It passed Mr. Moulton's cow, who stopped eating grass, which she rarely stopped doing, and looked up to see the riderless tricycle speed by.

It did not even stop at the trolley crossing, although the bells were clanging.

The brakeman jammed on his brakes, the conductor yelled "Whoa!" and the
passengers shouted "Stop!" The trolley came to a screeching halt just as
the tricycle crossed the tracks.

Dick, the conductor, jumped off muttering, "Good thing we had old number three-o-three out today or we would have hit it for sure. Good brakes. Crazy tricycle!"

He watched it roll out of sight heading toward Cape Porpoise. "Those fellows at the pier better watch out."

Sam was always at the Cape Porpoise Pier but he had never seen any-
thing like this before, a riderless tricycle wheeling by.  "Well I'll be," he
mumbled.

With nothing in its way to stop it, it rolled right off the pier.  Sam waited
to hear a splash but instead he heard a CRASH!  He looked over to see what
had happened.

With its wheels still spinning it had landed upside down on the stern of
Lee's lobster boat.  Sam called down, "Hey Lee, that's a funny looking
lobster you caught there!"

Lee motioned for the winch.  He hooked the tricycle by its front wheel
and had it hauled back up onto the dock.

A lobster boat was no place for a tricycle, but neither was a dock. Tom didn't want a tricycle around all the bait barrels and lobster traps.

With a sharp kick he booted it off the dock and on its way.

Back down Pier Road it went, around the mouth of the harbor.

At the Wildes Fire Station Alan exclaimed, "Bob! Bob! There's a tricycle coming down the road! And nobody's on it!" Bob aimed his fire hose at the tricycle, trying to stop it with the stream of water.

But instead of slowing down, the tricycle went even faster.

It headed down Ocean Drive, where Schepens-Kraus was painting a
picture at Blowing Cave.  She was so intent on her painting that she never
saw the tricycle racing toward her.

CRASH!  The painting flew one way, the easel another, and the tricycle
yet another.

Schepens-Kraus watched in disbelief.  First her painting fell upside down, then her easel.  The tricycle bounced once and finally landed on all three wheels.

As it rolled on down Ocean Drive, she thought, "That tricycle better watch out. The next time I'll grab it." Then she went back to her work and painted a tricycle rolling past Blowing Cave.

Jason's tricycle rolled on past a trash barrel, but this tricycle wasn't trash and didn't even slow down.  It wasn't going back to the dump.

It rolled past Mrs. Allen, who was stepping out of the Port Canvas Shop.
"Ah!" she shrieked, throwing all her bags and hats into the air.  Everyone
looked to see what was wrong . . .

Including Harvey. Out of the corner of his eye he caught sight of the
riderless tricycle as it turned the corner.

Lucifer, the black cat who lived up at the Book Port, was awakened by all
the commotion.  He was curious and came down to investigate.

As he turned the corner, he saw the tricycle coming toward him.

"Meeoooooow!" he shrieked.

Since Lucifer never went far from the Book Port he stared the tricycle out of
Dock Square.  He didn't go back upstairs to finish his catnap until he
saw it heading across the bridge.

Jason's tricycle wheeled along the waterfront, past the fishing boats and sailboats.

Art was painting a lobster boat when the tricycle bumped his ladder, knocking it out from under him. "Hey!" he yelled. "Who pushed my ladder down?"

Then he saw the tricycle rolling out of the boatyard, across the bridge, and toward a pile of trash. Before jumping down he shouted, "That's where you belong!"

It crashed through the trash that Butch, the rubbish man, had piled
next to his truck.

Butch grabbed his broom angrily and chased after the tricycle. It looked as though it might get away again, but it had slowed down just enough.

"Aha!  Gotcha!  I know just the place for a worn-out tricycle like you,"
Butch said as he carried it back to his dump truck.

"Up you go." And with a big toss Butch threw it to the top of the heap. Then he jumped in his truck and drove off toward the dump.

But Butch's truck hit a pothole and the tricycle fell to the ground while
Butch kept on driving.

Jason was looking for something to do. He hadn't felt like playing all
morning. He missed his favorite tricycle.

Suddenly, he heard a familiar squeak and then the sound of something bumping up the boardwalk.

"Here it comes, here it comes!" cried Jason.  "Here comes my tricycle!"  It didn't look worn-out to Jason.  It never had.  It looked worn in.

With one last bump it came to a stop next to the fire hydrant, right in front of him.

Jason's favorite tricycle was back.

# Acknowledgements

A great many people helped me in the making of this book. Among them are:

The unknown person who actually threw away the tricycle at the Kennebunkport Dump,

a model 861 made in 1953 by Junior Toy Corporation (now AMF Wheel Goods). See, it wasn't worn-out.

Jason Bastile and his parents, Jane and Jay;

Butch "The Trash Man" Welch; his wife, Priscilla, and all their children;

Ernest "The Dump Man" Julian; Custodian and one of many Executive Vice Presidents of the Kennebunkport Dump Association;

Forrest Moulton and his cows;

Dick "The Conductor" Perkins, Harold "The Brakeman" Ide,

Edward Frazier,

passengers Steve Brown and his father Sheldon, and the Seashore Trolley Museum;

Sam Wildes and the Cape Porpoise Pier Corporation;

Lee Hutchins and Tom West, "The Lobstermen";

Alan Wildes and Bob Boyd, "The Firemen";

Helen Schepens-Kraus, "The Painter";

Mrs. Francis 'Franci' Allen,

The Port Canvas Company, Tom, and all the employees: Paul, Neita, Linda, Jean, and Patricia;

Harvey Chick;

Lucifer "The Black Cat", Kevin Farley, Tom and Dottie, Jack and Shirley Fenner, and The Kennebunk Book Port;

Art Wester, "The Hanging Painter", and Brendze & Wester Traditional Marine Services.

Happy Dump Picking,


*Bruce McMillan*